the giver in me honors the giver in you.
xo. adrian michael

giver.

giver.
II

adrian michael

a lovasté project
in partnership with hwttbtw
published by
creative genius
CONCORDHAUS

Published by Creative Genius Publishing—
an imprint of lovasté

| Denver, CO | Concord, CA |

To contact the author visit adrianmichaelgreen.com
To see more of the author's work visit IG @adrianmichaelgreen
Book jacket designed by Adrian Michael Green

ISBN-13: 9798615409790

Printed in the United States of America

for the givers.
for those impacted by covid-19.
for ahmaud arbery.
for breonna taylor.
for george floyd.
for all black lives.

garden kisses x giveon.
tadow x masego.
toxic x kehlani.
cold war x cautious clay.
speak x jhené aiko.
roll some mo x lucky daye.
everything i wanted x billie eilish.
cherry hill x russ.
love x musiq soulchild.
i think i love you again x aaron taylor.
bigger x beyoncé.
rain x ro james.
i cry x usher.
float x 6lack.
feels good x jay wile.
think about me x dvsn.
bitter pill x christian kuria.
reason x 11:11.
i need x tgt.
last time x ro james.
tell me x usher.
90's r&b x famous.
need you x emanuel.
the letter x kehlani.
heartbreak anniversary x giveon.
moonlight x yo trane.

incense. palo santo.
tea. whiskey. wine. beer. water.

you are the reason. 1

you put yourself never. 2

in a room full of flowers. 3

sparkles. 4

you glow. 5

goat. 6

something marvelous. 7

lovely. 8

wait on love. 9

sunroom. 10

broken souls heal. 11

what it's like. 12

a great soul. 13

in helping them you help you. 14

find someone who is kind. 15

the serenest place. 16

what you've been through. 17

you enter souls silently. 18

palm trees and pools. 19

let what comes, come. 20

the cliffs of you. the coves of you. 21

summer on sundays. 22

the world in you. 23

approach with caution. 24

you are a river. 25

your own is you. 26

long distance love. 27

your love is contagious. 28

going to you. 29

when your soul writes. 30

pointing the moon back into you. 31

do not disturb.	32
uncut gem.	33
working heart.	34
dear teacher.	35
another flower grows.	36
where your ocean lives.	37
safe at last.	38
babysitting emotions.	39
when you silence yourself.	40
the cruelest of knots.	41
log into you.	42
a renaissance lives in you.	43
you and a day.	44
a givers love keeps going.	45
water tries to become you.	46
stand in your own wind.	47
more water than ocean.	48
sensitive moon.	49
a heart in your heart.	50
your love is dangerous.	51
all things beautiful and good.	52
evereverbeautiful.	53
the purest sunflowers.	54
yellow yellow.	55
sad soul.	56
inner inner.	57
you got this.	58
like a flame that never goes out.	59
looks fade.	60
dirty and sweaty.	61
dear soulmate.	62

old soul. 63

whirlwind. 64

slowly slowly. 65

peace or pleasure. 66

sometimes. 67

what remains and what goes. 68

better than any fortune. 69

forgive your old self. 70

yellow moon. 71

always always. 72

hard to love. 73

happy thought. 74

hope between the lines. 75

a kinder wild. 76

tradition. 77

you love different. 78

the one. 79

light can't see itself. 80

your type. 81

next time your feet tell your heart to run. 82

barefoot dream with lovely wings. 83

nothing can stop the sun from rising. 84

living wonder. 85

you are the moon. 86

you are always full. 87

we are all healing from something. 88

a close love you never have to question. 89

priceless and too worthy. 90

your lips are the dopest lines of poetry. 91

love has always been you. 92

maybe right now. 93

loving and leaving. 94

mad mud. 95

the risk and the reward. 96

love is cool. 97

the new you. 98

baby you deserve. II. 99

missing peace. 100

you are the one you're waiting for. 101

biting your tongue. 102

color of love. 103

if they leave while you change. 104

how you know someone is into you. 105

new moon. 106

four things you're entitled to do. 107

deep deep. 108

you roar of energy. 109

free spirit. 110

yours is yours. 111

stop accepting half love. 112

quiet chorus. 113

moon and wolf. 114

healing is in the love you give yourself. 115

go where your fullness is celebrated. 116

dear giver. II. 117

alchemist. 118

shelter in place. 119

fluency. 120

forever full. 121

you have this way. 122

the storm is you. 123

irreplaceable. 124

the best kind of humans.	125
four types of love you need.	126
this is how you know they don't care.	127
heart on lockdown.	128
the time is y:ou.	129
remove what doesn't serve you.	130
even your shadow is light.	131
let them deserve you.	132
moon eyes.	133
most authentic soul.	134
without the weight of someone else's gravity.	135
spread love.	136
unbothered.	137
unhide the hidden ones.	138
wildfire.	139
why they leave.	140
love is your crown.	141
the most beautiful human.	142
the best type of happiness.	143
nothing shallow is allowed near you.	144
your reach is beyond your control.	145
the greatest love.	146
attached.	147
twenty signs you're a beautiful giver.	148
let them go. keep yourself.	149
lace.	150
four flowers to give yourself.	151
peaceful love.	152
you are water.	153
the day before and the day after.	154
xo.	155

you are the reason.

you are the reason. but when was the last time you knew this. accepted this. breathed this. moved like this without undermining this deep truth. this commandment. this universal rhythm that foundations all foundations. you. are the tint between daylight and nightlight. you make anything that gets in the way of you suffer but not in the terrifying or harmful suffering. in the beautiful longing. beautiful desiring. beautiful wanting. beautiful inspiring. beautiful whying. beautiful rain. beautiful rain. beautiful rain. you. are. the. reason. the meaning. the final call. the natural tendency that opens eyes opens hearts opens minds opens dreams and awakes awakes awakes all who were once sleep. and keeps them alive. keeps them going. keeps them forward. keeps them excited and energized and healthy. to get up when they just want to still but they know being still when there is much to do gets them nowhere. gets them where nothing happens. stillness is necessary but not all the time. so you so you so you are the energy the fuel the adrenaline that hits their system and gives them what they don't even know they need. you are the reason the breeze breathes such softness such fierceness such reminders that is like water for the soul. water for the ocean. water for all the beings. can't you see. can't you feel your power. that power. right there. right there. don't lose sight of your reason. your you. your every every. every part. every essence. every crevice. every sound. every motion. be the reason you look to. be the reason you were made for. take in your reason. and orient. orient. orient. fall on yourself and feel feel feel the summer of your heart. the hues of your giving. the pull of your gravity. the depth of your well. hold your breath if you need to. everyone else does. everyone else does. you can breathe now.

you put yourself never.

you put others before you. always. always someone first. always
you last. sometimes you put yourself never. not in any place.
you see this as a weakness because you often beat yourself up
everytime you say this time will be the last time. but you aren't
you if you're not lifting someone up. their happiness matters most
to you. and that is what makes you happy. and by doing this)by
putting people before you(that is the rarest gift. it is what keeps
you honest. putting others before you looks good on you.

in a room full of flowers.

engulfed in a room full of flowers and you are the one centerpiece.
try as you might to avoid attention all eyes glance at you. you are
one in a million but the sun favors you.

sparkles.

every star in the sky
every single star
sparkles
flashes
falls apart and then
re-assembles
whenever
whenever
your eyes
look
in their
direction.

you glow.

you glow. you have this stunning about you. it must be the way your light hits and scatters across the room. everyone everyone wants to glow just like you.

goat.

you are the greatest of all time.

something marvelous.

goofy. silly. ridiculously humorous. there is something marvelous about someone who enjoys playing and not taking everything so serious.

lovely.

lovely
lovely
you are so fine
exquisitely beautiful
a dream come true
so rare to find
imagine what you look like
on the outside.

wait on love.

there are countless people you have yet to meet. they are waiting. anticipating. preparing. praying. meditating. manifesting. your arrival. your meeting. your acquaintance. and they are going to love on you so hard. love on you so much. love you the way you love. love you the way you deserve. just give it some time. be patient. eventhough you want this right now you can't force it or it won't work how it is written. how it is supposed to. the right ones will find you as soon as you stop looking. they will bump into you and it will be amazing. wait on love.

sunroom.

improves concentration
increases productivity
reduces stress levels
boosts moods
invokes calm
feels zen
you
are
a
sunroom.

broken souls heal.

it is often said that broken people break people and that hurt people hurt people. but broken people and hurt people know what it is like in the darkest of times. they know what to say and what not to say. how to listen and not disturb. to have no answer but know how to hold space for you to feel. there is no fast forward or diagnosis or judgement or desire to treat or fix. broken souls heal when they are ready to.

what it's like.

why do you love so hard?
because. i know what it's like
not to be loved at all.

a great soul.

a great soul knows what is beautiful and is not afraid to say so.

in helping them you help you.

when you feel down the best way to get yourself back up is in the reaching out and the helping of others. sometimes this is all you need. but it won't be as in your face. you will feel a sense of despair and called to always resolve it yourself but there will be a person close to you who is drawn to you that will verbalize their own need to get out of their head out of a funk out of a frenzy. answer their call. go to them. give them what you would give yourself. step away from you and step into them. for this is how you renew yourself. by being there for your person. in helping them you help you. whether that is a visit. or a day trip. or a red-eye flight. a sleep over. a kick it session. a brunch. a movie. hours on the beach. wine bottle and favorite snack. whatever it is it will be more than enough. a start on a path to getting out of and getting through.

find someone who is kind.

i hope they find you. someone who is kind like you. i hope they find you. amidst all the noise that is out there. i hope they find you. how could they not. you are a guiding light in a thick fog. i hope they find you. but sadly they don't know what they don't know. some souls are lost but swear they know where they are. but without you they are directionless. visionless. hopeless. i hope they find you. what buried treasure you are.

the serenest place.

you are the mirror of life. all one has to do is put their gaze on your temple and feel the past present and future all at once. you are the serenest place.

what you've been through.

what you've been through you've been through.
it's part of you but don't let it define you.
your best days are ahead of you.

you enter souls silently.

you enter souls silently
like a night hawk circling circling
if they were to see you coming
certainly certainly
they would retreat.

palm trees and pools.

palm trees and pools fill you. palm trees remind you of the crown you have on your head and pools remind you of the water inside you. you recognize yourself when you feel them come upon you. people recognize the royalty and the depths of you that they too can't help but picture you and summon you and think of you when both flow their way. when both flow their way.

let what comes, come.

let what comes, come.
let what goes, go.
you can't ride the wind
but you can always tell
which part of your face
it kissed and felt.

the cliffs of you. the coves of you.

they don't know or want to know all of you. they just want the
highlights of you. the first line. the last line. the heading. the
quick caption. they don't take their time and take you all in. and
what they miss)what they don't see(are all the nuances and the
most important pieces to you. if they cared more they would
halt and stop. stop. stop. and breathe you in. to give in to the
cliffs of you. the coves of you. the hidden figures of you. they
want to make it seem like they know you. the nooks of you. the
secrets of you. but they will have skipped the best parts of you.

summer on sundays.

you are summer on sundays. all days actually. with you days fade and forever go into nonexistence. you are open sky and bright moon. clear clear clear intoxicatingly clear. and beautiful. beyond that classification. for whatever reason beautiful was the word settled on but souls still are in search of a word a sound a phrase a meditation that will encapsulate you. so for now you're summer on sundays. a whole being to look forward to. some set calendars to specific months and dates and can't wait to pass the time to get to those moments. but you but you but you are warmth and moonlight on a daily basis. there isn't a hum that goes by without needing your feeling. needing your comfort. needing your you. summer on sundays. summer on all days. summer each second. summer. summer. summer.

the world in you.

always stay around people who want to do things. experience things. see how other people in different places around the world live and love and think. avoid don't do people. people who don't do anything except judge other people who do things. who gossip and cause drama. be in space with other dreamers. other souls who have creative imaginations who don't see the sky as the limit but sky as invitation. you already are the person who does great things. who goes where not many people want to. keep making your dreams come true. keep doing. because doing is far better than complaining. far greater than staying stagnant. far more interesting knowing there is so much domain out there waiting for you and other doers to visit. so don't be small)they want you to be small(and tucked away from the menu that is in front of you. and there will be opportunities you'll have to go alone. but you're paving the way. when people haven't seen what they've never seen possible by anyone close to them they stay shrunk and limited to what they know. can't blame them or shame them but this ain't you. you've always felt different from others with your need to break the mold. so go. and keep going. go out into the beyond and show that anything is possible. you're the kind of soul that has so much of the world in you.

approach with caution.

you want long-lasting and deep relationships. nothing that is fleeting ever filled you. so you approach people with caution. as you should. not just anyone can get a piece of your energy. you feel them out. as they feel you out. but not in a sizing you up situation. but in a are you for me conversation. you may seem reserved or holding back or in your head about them. but in actuality you are in your heart and in your patience seeing if you want to unlock the gate or not. because when you do there is no holding back. and all of you is laid out. your trust your love your everything is unleashed. your approach with caution is a warning. if they can't withstand a little rain they will never survive your thunderstorms.

you are a river.

you are a river
that winds
that winds
wrapping around
finessing through
shaping rocks
breaking down
flowing
flowing
you can't be stopped
you can't be stopped
you carry too much
without you
there is no life
there is no love
there is no nothing
you are water
soulful nourishing
water.

your own is you.

you used to be no good alone. alone frightened you. alone told you that you should have someone. to fill it. to fill you. but now but now you insist on time by your own side. by your own to refill a cup that you give your last drop. your own is you. a company everyone longs for. and you get to do this for yourself. a simple treat. for it was you that used to let the one you let in be the one to drive. to direct. to orchestrate. to decide. not because you had no voice no opinion no power but because you thought that was what a good heart a good lover a good partner did. to follow. to let. to accept their path as your path until it was time for your path to be walked on. but they just weren't really into where you wanted to go even if it was better. even if it would get them quicker and deeper than theirs. so letting that go letting that go letting them go found you looking for and stumbling back to you. back to where you were. back to where you always belonged. on you. in you. with you. to decide. to plot. to plan. to joy. to focus. to determine. where and when and why and who and how of you your life your heart. and no one no one no one can tame what was never meant to be tamed. it took the ship to capsize and for you to swim in the wreckage to find your air your wave your light. call it lost call it found call it whatever you are now where you are. better. golder. wiser. building. something. everything. and whoever turns your way can sense your vast your spacious your never leaving you again.

long distance love.

long distance love can exist with lovers in the same room. millions of miles gap you like a cavern insurmountable and no matter how much you try the hole widens. this is because one of you is trying. one of you is fighting. one of you is willing to close close close in hopes to get closer closer closer. but the other has made up in their heart that something else is much more important. much more priority. and you're at the bottom. to you i say this: don't give up on yourself. don't get down on yourself. don't think anything you have done or how you are or how you look is reason the one who said they care for you has checked out. give yourself permission to feel all the emotions and grieve in the gap of the love you once had. the love you want to have. claw one more good claw. cry one more good cry. tell them what will happen before you depart. and maybe)just maybe(they will snap out of their own selfishness and re-dedicate themselves. but if they don't)if they are too out of their heart(let them go let them go. pick up your heart. all of its whole and tattered pieces. shake your head. walk away with your soul intact. this long distance love didn't work. but a new love will come. a love that favors and lasts and works and gives as much as you give. you will never have to question that. a new road will take you to a love praying for you.

your love is contagious.

your love is contagious. it grows like wildfire.
one gentle parting of your light attracts souls.
there is no remedy to fight off what you give.
you are the cause and the cure. the kind that
sticks and lingers for five lifetimes. your love
spreads suddenly then all at once. they can't
escape or look away from a blazing hot sun.

going to you.

going to you is like homecoming.

when your soul writes.

i know your heart is hurting. and there are nights you cannot rest.
you turn on your phone and write down all the pain in your notes.
you try to get out what is coming up but the words the words seem
to fall faster than your hands can keep track. it's uncomfortable.
it's a process. this part of your life. but line by line you drop into
yourself. the self you've been avoiding.   you've wired yourself
in a way that is go go go. start up like. perpetually cutting off
emotions. keeping it business. transactional. and in the hustle of
stuff. of life. of bills. you're the last one who gets attention. and so
it is normal to feel like a bullet point. last on your list. so when
you pour it pours how you give in your day-to-day but in short
powerful messages you eloquently jot. your soul is crying. and it
may not flow in a sense. but it does serve a need. no matter the
order and no matter the words. when you allow yourself to flood
it will eventually come out. your heart hurts when you don't
do this. your heart heals when you give voice to your feelings.

pointing the moon back into you.

you want to share the delight you feel in your life but unsure who really is there who is really down who really will listen. and this bothers you because you want so badly to share but think it will come across as boasting. come across as inconsiderate. but barely you lift your accomplishments. your excitements. your upcomings. but stop quieting your joy. stop turning down what should be yelled and echoed to the top of the top and proclaimed as yours. as extension of you. as there is nothing ever wrong about talking about you. about sharing you. about pointing the moon back into you and praising all the work all the sacrifice all the dedication all the light you graciously serve the world. choosing yourself feels unnatural but see this is affirming practice as your soul simply watering itself.

do not disturb.

some from your past still want you. and they continue to reach out. they call. they text. they like what they see of what you post on social media. they send words and direct messages riddled with what they should have said way back when. way back when they had your attention. they deeply regret ever letting you go. and they won't leave you alone because you are still strong in their system. but you are not to be disturbed. at first you thought it was cute and cool now it's annoying and immature. they won't get the point. no matter how direct you are. so you don't respond. there is no need to give them attention. because when they had it they didn't know what to do with it. so stay on do not disturb. you won't see their notifications. their emojis. their subliminals. you can block them all you like but just like undesired things they still pop up. so keep doing what it is you are doing. loving where you are loving. loved where you are loved. your work is not to give anymore energy. any more rounds of reminding them of why you moved on. the past is in the past and it's no longer on you to teach them or show them or explain to them or plead with them or work with them on anything anymore. you're not that person to better them anymore.

uncut gem.

so many try
so many try
to pull
to extract
to take apart
you
from your
natural
state
your
wild
your
home
just so
they can
flaunt
and
take credit
for discovering
for conquering
for polishing
you
but you
but you
are an
uncut gem
and nobody
nobody
can claim
magic.

working heart.

being you can sometimes feel strange. every bit of you works
full-time. everything you touch turns to gold. everything you set
your heart on blooms. and you want to be everywhere all the time
so no one can say anything bad about you. even when you have
down time you are working overtime. checking in on people.
following up on other seeds you planted. other projects you
started. seeing if anyone needs help on anything. your
heart never quits. your heart never quits. this
is just you. who you are. but dear
work your heart a little
bit less. rest.
rest.

dear teacher.

you. dear teacher are a selfless giver. you are over worked and under paid. this is double the suffering. double the hardship. as you are needed and underappreciated. exponentially. all the invisible hours. the differentiation. the stations. the countless attempts to unveil the minds and open the hearts of our future. choosing to show up when you're extremely tired after only a few hours of sleep. leaving your classroom late just to come back early to do it all again and receive not one thank you not one mention not one accolade isn't why you do this work but it would be fuel. you. dear educator. are a champion. a giant. a hero. for giving and not expecting anything in return except the light to go off and sparks to emanate from those you teach. those you reach. those who don't know it yet but will eventually come back in person or in spirit to breathe life into your significance. into your pushing. into your inspiration. for without you they wouldn't be where they are or where they are soon to be. this isn't ego or flaunt. this is fact. you are a guide with special access to countless souls who just can't seem to always see their super powers. you are the reminder. the mirror. the springboard. the giver. who doesn't get paid enough for your calling. but paid enough each moment a student reaches for you. you and your service are appreciated. always.

another flower grows.

every time your name is recited another flower grows.

where your ocean lives.

you deserve so badly to be held how support beams hold homes. but like those beams you go unseen. behind the scenes. your love is up when everyone else sleeps. but even wide awake they overlook the moon. you're there aching wanting waiting to hear the sounds of a lover whisper in any articulation how much they love you. it is less about the words and more about how the syllables sync to your eardrum and slide to where your soul has been feeling so damn lonely. you haven't been visited down there in a long time. not. since the first time. because the first time is sometimes hard to re-create. so many people have assumed you wanted love in a certain form when all they had to do was ask you how to love you the right way. and here you are. just genuinely wanting to be cared for. reached for. loved for. kissed for. to swan dive under where your ocean lives. where calm lives. where magic resides. there is only one place to find you. they know where to search and rescue their own happiness if they just look out at who is right in from of them. you. are right there. right there. right. there. deserving so badly to be seen. to be seen. to be. seen. you are not hard to stumble on. they just can't see under water.

safe at last.

safe at last. that's what they say when they receive your love. when
they feel your energy. when they drop into your heart. safe. at. last.
what a vessel you are. for those who have never experienced a
soul like you. home is in your voice. home is in your hands. home
is in your walk. home is in your bones. all of that. all of you. is
the safety everyone needs and deserves. and you)too(need to
feel this way. find this way. in someone. not just in yourself. you
need touch and a person who emits complementary vibes that
creep down your spine and goosebumps your skin. to lean on and
feel with. not feel alone with all that you gift. when you find that
person who says:

> *finally. safe at last. you're safe with me.*

it will be worth it.

babysitting emotions.

you have tiptoed and played the political correct way of being nice. never wanting to come off as disrespectful or mean or unkind. so sometimes when you feel thorns brewing inside you because of what someone said or did to you you file it down. you break the sharps onto yourself. cutting you twice. suffering like a boiling pot with a too-tight lid. except your steam is well hid. but you have to be kinder to yourself. you can show your thorns but that doesn't mean you latch them onto anyone. there are ways to push back by letting someone know about themselves. by letting out what you have been holding in and not censoring your own emotions for the detriment of you but the benefit of them. no longer will you be babysitting emotions. to treat them like they can't handle what comes out of you. well guess what. if they have the courage to say and do what they want you have the courage, too. so figure out some come backs. some lines in your arsenal that immediately lets someone know what they said wasn't appreciated. that you're above their foolishness and won't stand for it any longer.

when you silence yourself.

your own standards should be what guide you. if you try to keep up with what others are posting what others are saying what others are pressuring then you have already lost. and this life isn't about winning or losing. it is about being. thriving. figuring. exploring. working to fulfill the soul not working to burn yourself out. and when you work out or when you buy expensive things or when you take that job or when you go to that college or when you charge that credit card or when you date that person or when you stay anywhere that doesn't feel right you may be digging in soil you have no business in. but the busyness of life filled with so much noise is about wondering if the soil you are in is what is meant for you. and hopefully you will ask the questions ask the whys ask the reasons. of yourself. for yourself. if you can't grow then let it be a no no. look out look out. but sometimes you won't know until you try it. until you visit. until you charge. until you collide. until you see with your own eyes. feel with your own heart. just always always always be prepard to have a talk with yourself. don't avoid yourself. you only let yourself down when you silence yourself.

the cruelest of knots.

every step you take will conjure thoughts from others. some will respect you. some will doubt you. some will applaud you. some will knock you. and some will fear you. and those that fear you have a mix of reasons but the one that presents the most disdain is if you fear yourself. and when you fear yourself it can shut down any possibility. so carry any fear you have of you with you. prove to yourself)not anyone else(that you can do anything while afraid. anything while your body withstands the cruelest of knots.

log in to you.

people want to see your cards. see what you are doing. stay-up-to-date and keep tabs. but you owe no one your every move. when you go off grid go off grid. let close ones know but go airplane mode. turn off every device and flee. go and do and be with whatever sets your soul on fire. take days if you can. take a year. if people need to reach you they will find a way. but you don't need any interruption to complete what is in your forefront. we get so caught up in needing to have direct access it can feel like there is no more privacy. no more self. no more room to just be. picture perfect is such a failing expectation. such a demeaning and despicable interruption to our day to day. so unplug and give no heads up. deactivate. log out and log in to you.

a renaissance lives in you.

there isn't a quote a poem a story a song that will perfectly fit you. and in your search for one the closest you will ever find is the one you have yet to write. but even in your attempt you will say you can never put it as eloquently as anyone else could. that is our own downfall. our assumption that someone other than ourself can understand us. that through them we see us. and although there is some truth to that)art has a way of doing this(you yourself are art. the most compelling blend of light and art. a renassiance lives in you. in all of us. we just have to excavate for it.

you and a day.

when was the last time you took yourself out. splurged on you.
took yourself out and were your own valentine. 366 days)that's
you and a day(no one can love on you the way you love on you.

a givers love keeps going.

what do you mean when you say i love you. do you mean the depths of you sees the depths of the one on the other end of your adoration. do you mean you would do anything. do you mean the sound of your voice and the break in your cries speak their language. your love is crystal clear. it is the width of the widest ocean and a billion times past the center of the earth. your love means daily commitment and daily devotion. hourly insatiability. moment after moment longing and pleasurable fulfillment. your love has suspenseful meaning. it is ever changing but never the same. the question is posed because a givers love keeps going. finds more and more ways to satisfy. more and more ways to give. more and more ways to improve.

water tries to become you.

the water
the water
reflects
and sees you
stares up at you
and runs up
your skin
dripping
upwards
turning on itself
rolling into your pours
trying to stay
trying to stick
trying to become
you.

stand in your own wind.

flex more. not to be cocky. not to be blunt. not to collect applause. flex because you can. spread your wings and show yourself how powerful and how mighty and how beautiful and how intentional and how mesmerizing and how resilient and how breathtaking you are. to earmark how far you have taken yourself from the last time you were down on yourself. flex and stunt and boast and head high and back straight and pose solid. flex on you. stand in your own wind. in your own moon. in your own galaxy. and say:
i am here.
i am here.
i am here.

more water than ocean.

more water than ocean.
more water than skin.
more water than human.

sensitive moon.

you need to merge with someone who knows you are easily
wounded and very sensitive. and vows to never hurt you.

a heart in your heart.

a heart in your heart. that is what you need. someone who gets you without needing to get you. someone who knows you without you having to explain yourself over and over and over again. someone that can make eye contact or hear the spice in your tone and know exactly what to do.

your love is dangerous.

your love is dangerous. that is why many avoid you. why many can't face you. because you expect a vulnerability and rawness that no one has ever required of them. to you this is bare minimum and shouldn't be so hard. shouldn't feel like pulling pulling pulling. it should feel like giving giving giving and devouring one another in the entirety of what will fruit from your love. but your love is dangerous. it holds the blueprint to a happiness just beyond where sight doesn't see. only the heart is key. and once there once there a blissful eternity. a blissful eternity. but they think you'll do harm. with all that desire to be plainfully bare. you strike fear so they decide to spend time where it is easy. but they will never experience your love. your love that warmly washes over and covers and settles and tastes like all the great tastes and then soothes all over. you soothe all over.

all things beautiful and good.

today you might feel like crap. maybe consecutive days before you've felt the same. so reach out your hand and touch your heart. skin to skin. close your eyes. breathe in. in this moment you are enough. in this moment you are you. no expectations from others. no reason to be anything else for anyone else. in these breaths you are the most important soul in the world. be with you. sit with you. stay with you. know each day begins with you. you aren't your hurt. you aren't your past. you aren't your mistakes. you are all things beautiful and good. all things beautiful and good.

evereverbeautiful.

you were born
devastatingly
beautiful
and one day
some heartbroken soul
interrupted
and told you
you weren't
and for far too long
)way too long(
you repeated that lie
lodged in yourself
convinced
convinced
that it was true
but
you are beautiful
always always beautiful
evereverbeautiful.

the purest sunflowers.

did you know
the purest sunflowers
grow from your mouth
everytime
you walk into your light.

yellow yellow.

all the colors are you. especially yellow. yellow yellow. it pulls in
and pulls out drawbridges in hearts and faces. yellow yellow. you.
on demand harvest of organic honey and sun. you are all the
blossoms and the bloomings and the becomings of energy.
your magic is inside of you. your magic is what love is.

sad soul.

anyone who shames another human for stepping into their confidence is a sad soul who needs their light restored.

inner inner.

by being yourself you can never fail. you have every right to be messy and imperfect and tinker and wonder. never hold yourself back because of a potential of something not working out. you are in the mix. you are your greatest equation. gather all the experience all the lessons all the missing pieces and depart. go. summon all that inner inner and trust you are everything and have everything)and more(to be successful. that inner inner is that charisma. that courage. that core. that creative. that crown. to embark into uncharted unknown unnerving that won't even know what hit them when you arrive. even if they knew you were coming no sort of preparation would matter. they have seen nothing or experienced anything or will know a love like you. trust your inner. trust your inner. trust your inner. don't question what was already written. all you have to do is step into your purpose.

you got this.

you got this. at least that is what you tell yourself with tears in your eyes. you keep going. and you take on the day. but there are breaks in you that breaks your heart and you want to stop but you can't fall apart. you need to be seen as the strongest and the baddest and the boldest. the one that is rock solid. but even rocks shatter. but you don't have to shatter you just need to let yourself feel a bit more. so let the tears fall. and the words hold you. even the sharpest sword needs water to keep it shiny and new. so care for yourself. you do got this. and all the oceans that come from you come back to you with more depth more salt more you.

like a flame that never goes out.

lovers like you work so damn hard and give as much as you can. those shoulders of yours have held so many people and your hugs your hugs are soft and full as pillows. remain proud of who you are and remain your beautiful soul. people flock to you when they need healing and you are always willing to listen. to give. to show you genuinely care. you leave a little of you with them. and they travel along with essence of you like a flame that never goes out.

looks fade.

looks fade
souls grow
beyond your beauty
inside shows
your values
your drive
your heart
)that wild heart(
it is your ambition
to always
focus
focus
focus
inward
and
hella
bloom
within.

dirty and sweaty.

getting under the hood of life and switching out old parts for new parts and getting your hands dirty never bothered you. grime and oil and mud and all that earth has to offer you dig into. scrub into. rolling around in the woods of life ignites you. you are the natural world. you are part of it. this is why you return to it. retreat to it. crave the outdoors. crave you. stay you. stay naturally. you.

dear soulmate.

you are what happy dreams feel like and you just want to hold on tight. the perfect match once striked it never goes out. you. there are never words. none that adequately come close to describe your soul. what is a prayer manifested. or the sound calm makes above the waves and under water. there was no mistake when we connected. how we fit and heal one another. how we stand in fire side by side. heart in heart. not letting go no matter. dear soulmate. gods of all races and cultures and traditions write about you. songs and sighs wail and speak your name. you are an entire love language wrapped in beautiful essence. your skin is your crown.

old soul.

new and flashy things don't excite you. you don't desire to be followed by photographers to capture all your highlights to share with the world. keeping things to you and your inner circle is what you hold dear. there is a kind of throwback style you keep intact. as if the more and more technology tries to control us you push back and keep postage stamps and envelopes for folks to get perfumed notes in the mail instead of instant messages that takes two seconds to send. privacy is your souls way of saying not everyone can have you at their fingertips at their screen at their convenience. this doesn't make you closed off it makes you an old soul. and old souls believe in chivalry. romance. and love. they still exist. because you exist and carry its tradition in every space you occupy. everywhere you go all the people that breathe you in get this feeling that you aren't from here. that you are of the old ways. the old generation. a time where in order to get a hold of someone you either left a voicemail on their home phone or had to drive by and see if they were inside. a time where playlists were burned on blank cds. marked up with sharpie that got scratched real bad because you played the disc too much. you're the kind of old soul that still plays songs to your lover over the phone. sends them songs to listen to on their way home. old souls give the best and deepest love. it seeps and seeps and seeps until it finds your soul collides and twirls and ties itself. soul ties last longest. those bonds can never be untethered or broken. fall in love with an old soul and your heart rate will forever race. you will fill alive and feel the sweetest tenderness. the sweetest tenderness.

whirlwind.

right now it isn't about anyone else. you need it to be all about
you. this is another reminder to make it happen. you may not have
done it the last time these words nudged you to. but whirlwinds
like you need your own air, too. need to take in the colossal stature
that is you. not sure where you feel your heartbeat the deepest
but be sure whoever you last gave it to doesn't have it on layaway.
isn't simply saying all the right things as incremental payments
but has earned and invested and is dedicated to loving you. you.
whirlwind. you know how it feels to saturate and expend all of
what you have in order for others to be full. you sometimes are the
last one to eat and the first one to clean. the last one to get to bed
and the first one to get up. the last one to be doted on and the first
to show up with gifts. but don't spin yourself out. spin yourself in.
re-charge. re-charge. re-charge. for you can't help that yours is
the wind people seek. yours is the wind that magnifies and lifts
lifts lifts the wings of others. they can't fly as high without you.
nowhere near the heights you get them to.

slowly slowly.

before you get up. before you get up. sit for a bit. rest another tick. i know you want so badly to re-start where you may have left off or begin a new urgent errand. but start this one slowly slowly. if you jump out of bed don't. ease yourself up. ease yourself out. get to the edge where your feet can feel planted and take in some deep breaths. slowly slowly. outstretch your hands and bend your back. curve to the side and roll your neck. side to side. slowly slowly. crack your body your joints in places tension holds. slowly slowly. stand when you're ready. walk. to wherever you need to first go. walk. sigh. release. brush. shower. use cold water if you can. set your intentions with yourself as you get time with yourself. alone in your thoughts. your time. your time. slowly slowly. continue your routine. make way make way and smile more than you often do. practice gratitude in your mind in your heart. brew. cook. read. eat. slowly slowly. and if there are others in your household who step into your practice your routine welcome them. show them what slowly slowly looks and feels and sounds like. and before you have to do whatever you have to do. try changing in your mind that you *get* to. you get to go somewhere. or you get to meet someone for coffee. or you get to change their diaper. or you get to walk your dog. you get to go to work. you get to do certain things even if you don't want to and can feel like obligation. it is a matter of switching up and bringing to it yourself. slowly. slowly. at your pace.

peace or pleasure.

are you chasing peace or pleasure. are you filling time with what serves you or further cuts you off from what you should be doing. you provide both peace and pleasure. but know the ones who seek you may not want both. they mainly want you for pleasure. or they mainly want you for peace. up to you on who)if either(is what you want to be a resource for. do you give yourself peace. do you give yourself pleasure. you can be both. you should be both. in whatever capacity of your choosing. but too often many have treated you just as a pleasure pit stop. picking from you from their emptiness and left until they needed a re-fill. too often humans do this to one another. pulling up knowing they plan to peace out once they get their pleasure fix. then act like nothing happened. meant nothing. but you are more than a fix more than a shot more than something to be taken. you are the combination and the secret. the path of righteous existence. see you. you carry inside you the nectars that make all who deserve your peace your pleasure discover an endless bliss. a heartfelt zen. a profound love.

sometimes.

sometimes you find lessons. sometimes you find love.
whatever you find in a person. whether that be long term or short
term. there's a reason your paths cross. don't get in the way by
rushing what is or isn't meant to be. cherish each moment. you'll
know what is meant for you when it arrives. you'll know who is
meant for you when they arise.

what remains and what goes.

you weren't ready or expecting or bracing yourself for a fraction of the tough shit that you have been through. that has hit you. that has come to your door step. that has made attempts to rattle you. but you. you were built and fastened and designed and prepared for whatever came your way. like a ship knowing the waves soon will rise high enough to break its way onto its deck. and you. are made of the stuff that lasts. the stuff that stays. the stuff that isn't easily destroyed. what comes to you makes you more impenetrable. for what is meant to challenge you doesn't frighten you. yeah sometimes you desire to be the soft rather than being the hard but your softness allows and brings about your hardness underneath. where most wall themselves allowing no light in. you are the light in which terrifies difficulty and pain and anguish and hurt and harm and sadness. yet you know all of this is part of life. not opposite of or better than positive emotions you know that all that comes is part of the journey. what matters is what you let stick to your soul. that you decide what remains and what goes.

better than any fortune.

it is true what they say. that when things change inside you the things change around you. a spiritual thing. you are a spiritual being drapped in beautiful skin. and although there are others around you that aren't ready for a deeper reflection this can never stop you from your connection. your need to smile without smiling. as you get more comfortable with your self the more of your own magic can't help but fall out of your mouth. you plant seeds in the bodies of everyone around you. physically. digitally. and then you activate them. not in word per say. but in the way only you understand. and people may never admit it)it is what it is(but you provide so much love better than any fortune.

forgive your old self.

forgive your old self. you were just making room for the you that now sits on the throne. you aren't one for excuses but you were young and didn't have the language that you have now. the tools and resources that you are right now. thank your younger self. thank your younger self. thank your younger self. thank. you.

yellow moon.

the sun is happiest when you shine.

always always.

you are all brain and all beauty. one hundred percent both. it is quite surprising. but you aren't surprised. you know this about you. it is the doubters and people who wish to know you who have created a false narrative in their head that people who look like you and sound like you and dress like you and love like you and dance like you and boss like you and energy like you can't be standing and vibing and rocking the way that you do. they model themselves off you. try to take from you. make game plans based off you. and by the time they think they have you figured out you have left that old skin and became another greater version of you. you brain. you beauty. you all. are the destiny and they will always always always always always always always always always look to you for the answer and give you none of the credit.

hard to love.

you aren't hard to love. whoever tells you that or implanted that in your mind just has no idea how to properly describe a gem. you are just so damn rare and hard to find. hard to convince to lower your standards. hard to pull the wool over your eyes. but the hardest part about you isn't that you are hard to love. the hardest part is leaving your side. even if for a moment. even a instant before a blink can be complete. the hardest part of you is matching your compassion. and having the sweetest heart like you. too many pretend to care but your care is never an act it is the living and breathing and being that you are. you are only hard to love)to use what they say(because sadness caused in you is unbearable and you deserve a love that will plunge into sadness before sadness has a chance to reach you. that they hold up the weight of a tear and ask your permission if you want to give it an audience or push it back in. this isn't about unconvincing you that you aren't hard to love. because you are. but not in the way they say it. not in those negative terms. i get where they are coming from. but they are just too lazy to work for your attention.

happy thought.

where is your time. and where do you place your mind. it's always in the good places but sometimes saying it out loud forces you to remind yourself that you always always always are your very last happy thought.

hope between the lines.

when all looks devastating and glib
there is you
when pitch white is too blinding
there is you
when the sky parts become sand parts
there is you
when comets crash into themselves
there is you
when breath loses its shape
there is you
when shadows become invisible
there is you
when steps are retraced
there is you
when fog departs
there is you

you
are
hope
between
the
lines.

a kinder wild.

you are constantly changing. choosing a direction that feels
right by heart and less by sight. you trust. you trust. you trust.
without needing to see the end of a road. in tunnels dark you are
more curious than you are worried. the only worry that crosses
your thought is worry you might get through to the end too fast
without properly experiencing the challenge. not because you
want things that are difficult. but because nothing worth having
should be too easy or else once you have it there isn't much trying
that will keep your attention. and even if you change direction
your destination remains the same. headed towards a better
version. a better situation. a kinder wild.

tradition.

gratitude is a love language
you've always practiced.

you love different.

you love different. souls as old as yours are like the sea. timeless.

the one.

you are the one. the one that somebody sighs for. the one that
moon rotates for. the one that skycrapers emulate. you. are the
one that has angel dust in your bloodstream so from time
to time your body tightens just to remind your skin you're just
down on earth visiting. you. are the one that light beams from.
your best side is inside. in you are castles on clouds and rose
gold lines the crown that follows your shadow. you are the one.
harps cry and yearn for. i'm sorry what keeps you up keeps you
shackled to the idea that something about you needs fixing.
but those who need fixing are the very ones who pass their own
poison just so it tastes better spewed on you. but you are not
the one. not in this season. not in this chapter. not in this stage.
to keep down toxins inside you sheltering it calling you home.
no. their lies aren't yours to house no more. no. the sickness
they gave you has outstayed its terrorism. you are the one.
have always been the one. to absorb what isn't yours and carry
it for others. you've learned that their load isn't welcome and
although remnants of their thorns still try and cut you they
aren't strong enough to disrupt your healing. and although
you experienced hardship you are the one rising through
the ashes. coming out more beautiful. more resilient.
more love and light. more new. the one rose
who grew out of concrete and became
fearless and bold.

light can't see itself.

light can't see itself. tell yourself this the next time there are waves
of days that fill your spine with aches of disbelief of the rare light
that is you. some days you roll with your rays head high crown
on twenty out of ten. but other days you struggle to find your way.
struggle to see what i see. rare light. beautiful rare light. the
greatest kind. you just need to remember that light can't see itself.

your type.

your type is the type artists write poems and songs about.

next time your feet tell your heart to run.

stay.

stand.

breathe in the heat.
this is how dragons
sharpen their tongues.

barefoot dream with lovely wings.

you're an intoxicating kind of beautiful.
everything about you creates a swelling.
a rapid. a peace. that's because you are
grounded in the aura of you. no filter.
no pretend. no trying to be someone else.
you've always been you. charming. bright.
you're a barefoot dream with lovely wings.

nothing can stop the sun from rising.

you don't just grow. you glow. you show.
and some can't stand to see your shine. so.
what. let that go. keep going. keep. growing.
and being. and being. and being. for if you
stop for anyone's sake but your own you'll
never forgive that part of you yearning to
wild the way wild is supposed to be. freely.
don't doubt that fire within you burning.
that voice telling you to face the shadows
is inner strength. listen. ignite you. nothing
can stop the sun from rising. so rise. rise. rise.

living wonder.

that heart of yours is made of gold.
always has and always will be. some
people just don't know how to handle
or treat or care or appreciate a living
wonder. don't get down or cover up
your golden love. don't do that.
the one for you would never
be foolish enough to see
you as anything other
than the greatest
purest gift.

you are the moon.

the most incredible thing about you
)there are so many(is how sincere and
trustworthy and kind you are. despite
how cruel others can be towards you.
don't change. never substitute that big
unparralled exceptional glorious heart.
for it is as if the universe chose you
chose you specifically out of them all
to be the one. to be the only one.
the one we see. up high. high. high.
way up there. spot lit. star bright.
did you even know. did you.
that you. that you.
are the moon.
the inspiration.
the entire tide and
puller of feelings out
out out of chests and blasts
old ways of thinking
making and clearing space for
the new world you implant effortlessly.
for you are such a soul whisperer.
and you and only you sense the waters
in others. how do you do that. how. how.
secrets of the moon.

you are always full.

don't let someone
fill you because they
think you're empty.
you are always full.
more whole. more
complete. in ways
they will never
ever know.

we are all healing from something.

we are all healing from something traumatic from our childhood. you'll be surprised when you dig into some of your behaviors and see how you treat others, or how your tolerance level of how others treat you mirrors an upbringing you still carry in you. with you. emotional hurtings show up in relationships when you seek to be fulfilled or want so badly to be seen and appreciated but it temporarily or doesn't even fill a bucket. you don't accept love because you've never seen what healthy and unconditional love looks like. when you start peeling back and healing and telling yourself)and believing(what was withheld from you wasn't your fault, you'll begin to see patterns and change how you see a love you have always needed and always deserved.

a close love you never have to question.

when they ask you
how was your day
and let you talk
for hours
without interruption
except with bright eyes
and deep deep smile
is the kind of intimacy
you deserve
this is a close love
you never have to question.

priceless and too worthy.

your worth isn't up for negotation. you are priceless
and too worthy to lose. there is no bargaining in-between.

your lips are the dopest lines of poetry.

your lips are the dopest lines of poetry.
part them and entire oceans rise. touch
them and hearts catch fire.

love has always been you.

it's okay to be alone. you don't have to fill your time with people or conversations or behaviors that draw you away from yourself. you can enjoy yourself by yourself and let you time be the best time. doesn't mean you're lonely or make you alone. sometimes you gotta focus on you. and notice every moment you try to reach for someone or something else to get out of a discomfort to tell you something about yourself. you may be used to being surrounded with their noise. other noise. not your noise. you may be blasting yourself out. take a break from people and appreciate the soul within.

what a treat you are to your own life.

feels good. to just be. doing what fills you. what energizes you. you and time. and your own devices)not tablets or phones(. just you. to cheers yourself. to wine yourself. to drive yourself. somewhere. somewhere.

and there will be times your solitude fills
you up better than any person ever could.

they taught you that you needed someone else to make love to you to feel loved. but they didn't know that love is you and you.

love has always been you.

maybe right now.

maybe right now they do not long for you.
maybe right now they do not need you.
soon. soon. the tides will turn and they will
yearn for what they should have considered.
should have believed in and loved on right
from the start. their mind will get over you
but their heart will always always cry out for you.

and you will be their biggest regret. their mind won't let them
believe it but their heart will never let them forget you.

and the one who knows from the start will never let you go.

that's the person you hold onto.

the one that sees you in their future as soon as you speak your
name. as soon as your souls dance for the first time. as soon as
your heart races to the car and the first to call shotgun. love is in
the little things.

at your favorite bar at your favorite booth smeared on your
favorite menu or worn out vhs movie.

if you think love is big big big and what was written on screens
you can keep that imagination but you'll miss it when it shows you
true love is far from a director's cut.

when you re-define what love is. you'll find it. you'll find it. they
will find you. they will find you.

loving and leaving.

loving and leaving are the same.
both require choice and commitment.
you just have to decide which hurts more
and which hurts less.

whoever hurt you did a real number on you.
they messed it up for the one who gets your heart.
but not everyone can handle fire.

mad mud.

you aren't mad or crazy or out there. not in the way they say you are. your kind of mad and your kind of crazy and your kind of out there is a balanced mixture of you and the wind. you and the stars. you and the water. you and the countless freckles dabbled on your body. just because you venture to add to your strengths and your abilities by way of your own mud doesn't make you anything but beautiful. more beautiful. beyond beautiful. infinitely beautiful. it is your truth that without mud there is no lotus. no bloom. no you. so yes. be mad. be crazy. be out there. dive into your own chaos and inspire others to do the same. for the hellfire and holy water that boils through you is the very nutrients that fuels your soul. and when they call you mad ask them how mad. and when they call you crazy ask them how crazy. and when they call you out there ask them how out there. because they don't know what that means. they don't know the depths of the mud you tread in. they don't know how you blossom the way you blossom. as it is impossible to just bloom once. you are everblooming. so dear mad mud. stay mad. stay crazy. stay out there. stay blooming. you are the blueprint of what gold dust is made up. particles of wings and wild and magnetic energy that tells you that you belong no matter what other people say. the giver in you chops up all that might be negative and converts it into positive. and the system you do this through is your own version of photosynthesis. yoursynthesis is by simply smiling. the light enters your eyes and your mouth and through every pour on your ocean. everything you touch turns magic. you make what may feel horrific feel bearable. that's that warrior spirit flow. that indigo trait. that doesn't find shortcuts but finds courage to demonstrate. the only thing you understand is effort and reciprocity and giving and love. and that if they aren't willing to get in the mud with you they are the ones truly mad.

the risk and the reward.

you are worth fighting for. in this lifetime and the next. and the million lifetimes you exist after that. for choosing to fight for you is the smartest thing anyone could ever do. who wouldn't do anything to savor you. or stand by you. or just be whatever you need just like you are whatever they need. fighting for you shouldn't be hard or questioned or delayed. it should be instant. not because you need anyone to fight your battles)you can defend your own title(but because any distance from you is too far away and every day someone gets to be close to you is the best of all days. so any time they strike a match that disconnects you and you begin to fizzle away, they better strike another match to bring you back. or losing you would be the deepest heartache they will ever experience. you are the risk worth taking. to do anything for. to cherish and to love. the reward worth striving towards. not to possess but to protect. to keep from harm. there are too many someone's who will try to stand in your way and in your light and whoever holds your heart should vow to never intentionally be one of them. staying and lasting is the fight. is the dance. is the rumble. any relationship wanting to go far must be in the trenches. to withstand and take on anything. alongside you. the willing. the ready. the always. and anyone uninterested in the work)love is never easy(should never step to you in the first place. you're not the one to take things lightly. you ride fierce and determined and commit and loyal and defend without flenching. that's just you. and not getting any of that back is a shame because you are more than worth fighting for. you are a chance at love forever. and if they miss your landscape they will only ever see in portrait. and you are by far wider and deeper than any love in existence. that ever occupied breath. and the true fighter that understands this chance and you grant access to your heart can't mess this up.

love is cool.

love is cool.
but love
without action
ain't shit.

the new you.

the old you would stay out of consideration of others. the new you leaves spaces that take you for granted. not everyone should have access to you. your talents. your heart. your love. notice how you feel around people. trust your intuition. you know when you are being used and when you are being appreciated.

baby you deserve. II

a lover who makes you forget what
others made you feel insecure about.

someone willing to put their heart on the line and
open up just as much as you are vulnerable with them.

a lover who sees you
as their one and only.

someone not just down to say they will change.
someone who notices what pains and changes.

a lover who waters every wound with loving speech.
a lover who gives deep love unconditionally.

someone who has more than you need.
someone who has and gives and gives and gives.

a lover to grow with.
a lover to heal with.

someone who doesn't see you as their rehab. as their dumping
ground. as their recovery. as their rebound. as their temporary.

a lover who lasts unlike the others. who dedicates. rededicates.
commits. recommits. every day. vows. revows. stays. doesn't leave.

missing peace.

it's okay if you aren't okay. not feeling your best. dealing with so
much stress. so much tension in your body. up late and can't sleep.
it's okay if you're not all put together as you normally are. but
nothing is normal during these times. you're going through a deep
cleansing and keeping it together really means allowing yourself
to fall apart and see yourself in pieces. you're strong enough to
re-assemble yourself. you are your own missing peace. relax your
mind. you are loved you are loved you are love.

you are the one you're waiting for.

you are the one you're waiting for. people will come and they will go. but you. you will stay. you can't leave yourself. there were times you did leave yourself for others. and it was fine. it was choice and choices have a way of showing the results far later down the line and you can't always rely on deciding what to do based on the future that doesn't exist yet. so)as you always do(you prioritized others in hopes to be prioritized later. but later never came. and here you are. still in the clouds. but these clouds are your own. for you. holding you. evaporating you. elevating you. reminding you. that you make your own weather. that you are the storm and the sun. the knight and the distressed. you are everything you have been searching for and overlooked. the royal servant and the sovereign. you and you are ready to be the one you have prayed about and hoped for and closed your eyes for and wished for and pleaded for and sacrificed for and wondered for and the wait is already over. you have been there all along. alone you have never been because you were with you it's just easy to forget ourselves. so there you are. look at you. beautiful strong courageous you. been armoured up and ready to champion others when in all actuality the armour has been for you. to battle for yourself. to stand for yourself. to love for yourself. this doesn't mean you aren't going to be there for others)you'll always do and be that person(but it's okay to be the frontline for yourself. to wait as long as you need until you realize you have always been the one. just don't wait too long to understand you are what you need. that you are the full moon and the full soul and the full love you've poured into others. pouring into them is pouring into you. fills you. completes you. you are complete. for you have always always always been the main source. you just were looking outward instead of inward. so look in look in. mirrors can't see their own beautiful reflection.

biting your tongue.

biting your tongue
for the sake of others
doesn't mean you're
weak or timid or passive
it takes more strength
and powerful energy
to hold back fire
than it does to let it go.

color of love.

love is in the starting over and beginning again.
don't you ever be afraid to believe that. love never quits.
it comes back.

you thought it would be forever. but it wasn't. it was what it was.
it knocked you because you tried to make it work. you had to start
over. you have to start over.

it's in the starting over where the fear of everything is. fear will
grip you into thinking you'll never be the same again. you are
right. you won't. you'll be better. fresher. open. sensitive. receptive.
love never leaves you because you are love. the color of love. the
shape of love. you just have to believe it for yourself love.

it is in the getting back up and putting yourself out. you may be
heartbroken again. but maybe you won't. that is the dance. the
invitation. to never give up. love never quits. you shouldn't either.

if they leave while you change.

if they leave while you change
they weren't meant to take part
in your full metamorphosis.

everyone won't last. but you'll be with you. and i hope
)for their sake(they stay. for you in full bloom is raw magic.

change on you
looks like
heaven
)if heaven
had a face(
every second
you're shifting
micro
growing
diving deeper
into your own
higher self
i just hope
that mountain top
applauds for you
the way i will always
always
always
be supporting
there there
by your side
regardless
regardless.

how you know someone is into you.

they tell you words you have never heard.
back up every line with loving action and
consistently check in on you. most people
don't like being bothered but messages and
moments from them don't feel bothersome.
they feel like genuine care because you are
nothing but authentic. and anyone who
gets even the smallest dose of your smile
knows you're not like anyone else.
they are into you because you know
who you are and light only reflects light.
if they observe closely they will never miss
your sunrise or sunset. eventually you notice
who stands on your sand versus who basks
in your ocean. the one for you)the one truly into you(
sees you like no one else. honors you with water and light.

new moon.

you are a new moon
in the arms of the old one
evolving yet never forgetting
where you grew from.

four things you're entitled to do.

create boundaries.
ignore people that bother you.
make mistakes.
go where it feels like home.

deep deep.

they will look for you in the wrong place.
thinking you'll be in shallow waters.
but you're deep deep miles underground.

you got that deep love. too many don't know how to hold
their breath. if they knew you they'd know you're deep deep
underground. the deepest water. where you're sometimes cold
and sometimes cool but always a perfect kind of warm that
hits you quickly leaving you wanting to taste some more.

you roar of energy.

light looks at you and says:
how do you do that. how how. you roar of energy.
you inspire me. you inspire me.

thinking of you.

how too often you think no one looks to you. aspires you. seeks
you. how you see others being reached for and affirmed and
desired. but look. look.

you're brighter than most. but you're too humble to see yourself
)remember light can't see itself(. i'm repeating myself. but saying
something at least seven times you'll finally let this sink in.

you are the light that merges sea and sunset. where breeze meets
bird. where heart meets love. light copies you. light checks you out
to see what to do. light goes off your scale. off your energy.

so many do the same. they look towards the light.
but little do they know they are looking at you.

free spirit.

you are a free spirit. young at age. old at soul. if something or someone doesn't hit your spirit you don't go near it. that isn't selfish or closed off. that is what free spirits are all about. you don't need permission to follow certain rules you have your own guide book embedded in your energy that flows with what feels good and whatever direction freedom goes in. your heart is vintage art. too much for some and just right for you. not looking for anyone to free spirit with. sometimes that life feels a bit lonely. but when you come across souls who get you, you're soul tied forever.

yours is yours.

there are days you aren't sure about anything. who you are. why you are. where you are. how you are. you're not always supposed to know. maybe. just maybe. uncertainty is okay. you don't have to be put together. perhaps unsolved questions will be what drives you to appreciate more. what gives you permission to just be still. be you. a work in progress. you don't have to be together. you don't always have to know. you don't have to stick to a plan. it's okay if you don't know how you feel. you'll figure it out. and maybe you won't. it's less about knowing fully and more about paying attention. don't think that everyone else knows what and why they are doing what they are doing and are secure in who they are. everyone is on their own path. everyone has their own truth. and yours is yours. so who you are and where you are and why you are doesn't need justification or comparison. just take a step take a breath and be. for being whoever you are is the knowing. is the wonder. is the question. and maybe all this life is about is the pursuit of more questions and less answers. less answers. less answers. maybe. maybe. may. be. you.

stop accepting half love.

you will notice how peaceful your life is when you stop accepting half love from people who pretend to care.

quiet chorus.

everything you do is amazing. everything. every. thing. how is that possible. that's like asking the moon how is it that every night it illuminates brighter and hits the soul deeper. your amazing isn't brag or boast or stuck up or conceited it is honest and down-to-earth. down-to-do-anything. that kind of chill that body feels all over. every thing you are is outstanding. alluring. endearing. reassuring. as if your love was meant only for the one you drop it into. making them feel like the only soul in the world. that thing you do)how you do it(can't be pinpointed. it is subtle. you are subtle. nothing about you is flashy or hinges on the desire to be honored publicly. you are a quiet chorus that harps and fills an entire cathedral with beautiful sounds that welcomes and homes any being with ribcages full of hearts not accepted anywhere else. what is most amazing is the maze of you. the puzzle of you. the more than one way to discover the vibrations of you. while some block off and ignore and distance certain types of people you are open and interested and do not discriminate love that comes your way. you never know who is meant for you if you keep going after the types that always let you down. people easily are drawn to you because of that smile that shows you are just like them. anxious and willing and human enough to try and harmonize. you never know. the one in the section you'd never hear or see may be who closes their eyes and breathes the sounds of you. can you hear it. they can hear you. it isn't loud or piercing or throbbing. you are a whole other wavelength. a whole other key. whatever belongs to you won't be long coming to you because goodness is always on it's way towards you. you are purpose. you live on purpose. you love on purpose. you give on purpose. you affirm on purpose. you gather on purpose. you activate on purpose. you manifest on purpose. you selfless on purpose. this is why you are amazing.

moon and wolf.

full of more than sunshine you are a combination of moon and
wolf. you are magic magic. a mood mood. a warrior at war for
love. fighting for what your believe. not backing down.

healing is in the love you give yourself.

healing isn't always in the stitches or casts.
splints or bandage wraps. sometimes there
is nothing that covers the walking wounded
better than gentle smiles of strangers and
the grace of those who may not understand
but have the willingness to sit and listen.
no desire to fix or afix judgement. healing
is in the carrying on when you just want
to carry less. healing is in the love
you give yourself. you can be hurt
and still face the world. you are
brave and inspire others
to do the same.

go where your fullness is celebrated.

you are strong. the strongest of strong. but you too are soft. softest of soft. you are both. always been both. that's how your love reaches. it lasts and withstands. waters and waters and waters. you are where all the beings go to get the best love. the sad part is some just dip into you when it serves them. and do nothing to pour back. examine that. reject those takers and go where your fullness is celebrated.

dear giver.

thank you. for holding. for creating space.
listening. connecting. covering and loving.
people have always needed you. always.
but now more than ever they flock and
download their stuff to you while you
try and keep yourself together. the
heaviness of all of this. you are
beyond incredible but take
no credit. but please care for you.
your mental and emotional
and physical wellbeing, too.
please. please. you can't give
from an empty well. so rest. and
unpack the weight of the world, too.
you deserve so much love for all you do.

alchemist.

you just know what to say and how to say it and when to say it.
how. how. only the magic ones. the givers. the mindful ones.
have this kind of quartz in their soul. it's like you're underneath
skin of every human being who needs healing. you get close
without physically being close. your energy lands and cuts
through any wall someone tries to put up but they are
no match to that magician in you. that alchemist
in you. that healer in you. my. my. my. what
guru you are. this is not your role. this
is your calling. your purpose.
embrace your magic.

shelter in place.

you are a kind of love that is least expected.
you are a kind of love that comes out of nowhere.
you are a kind of love that swarms and blindsides.
you are a kind of love that spreads more love.

but sometimes that kind of love isn't in plain sight. not anyone can just get it. can just get you. you are not to be gotten. you are to be respected and deserved and earned and honored and watered and spotlighted like the moon. not because you need center of attention. that isn't you. but because you're always there. you've always been there. some people just intentionally avoid looking up. for fear they may not live up to your magnitude. but your love is far from intimidating or daunting or reserved for a select few. you've just learned the importance of being enough for you. to be the love you always wanted so no one could ever say you didn't love them or love yourself. if some can't see you that isn't because you aren't around. they know where to find you. you aren't waiting to be caught or waiting to be saved or waiting to be swooped up. you are living. wandering purposefully. intentionally. meaningfully. out in the world. out in yourself. you are a shelter in place. a home. a giving space. a blueprint for what the world needs more of. you teach others that focusing internally is beautiful journeying. this is the real reason they avoid your moonlight. reason they say they don't know where you are or say they do not know where you have been. you are a reminder of self care. self worth. self wondering. you are the most powerful resource. your innerview terrifies others for what they may uncover in themselves. a longing in themselves. far too many souls stay away from their own home thinking fulfillment is elsewhere. if they were to stay and sit and be within. they'd find your kind of love.

fluency.

by now
if someone
isn't fluent
in your
love language
you're in
the wrong
relationship.

forever full.

fall in love with a giver and
you'll never go hungry for love.

you have this way.

the way you frequency you vibrate higher. naturally. easily.
whatever you put your mind to it happens. it manifests. you have
this way. untouched. untouchable. protected. it is your own.
your own holy place. tucked. deep. down. covered. somewhere.
only you know. you tap into it even in public. sitting across from
others. sitting amongst yourself. to peace. to calm. to zen. to flow.
as if no one can disrupt your high. your light. your energy. those
really close to you can sometimes see you when you do this. but
it is so subtle they often miss it. because your magic is your breath.
your inhale. your lovehale. people lucky enough to breathe you in
never tasted air like you. most people give off toxins. nothing toxic
about your way. your frequency doesn't allow for it. thank you
for your equilibrium. your everything. your emissions.
you radiate and don't hear this enough. xoxoxo.

the storm is you.

the storm is you. when you erupt or when you tranquil or when
you in-between. all storms aren't bad. most are needed. essential.
to water and replace. to test and practice and deliver parts of you
back to you. for you are the eye of it. in it. within it. all of it.
blasting and raining. rejuvenating. planting. replenishing.
collecting and harvesting. setting and resetting boundaries. see.
when you storm)you are always storming(there is this false
narrative that you're too intense. too fierce. too strong. those that
say this have no business near your winds. you can't be someone
else's wind and be expected to never gust. to never expand.
to never power. those intimidated by you just want to be you.
become the waves that crash up against your skin. be the moon
that pulls the tide of you. but you can't live tiny just for the sake of
another weather system seeking attention. no. keep you. be you.
stay you. storm and storm and storm and storm and storm and
always remember your best resource is your own source.

irreplaceable.

impossible to replace. that is you. although some may say you
are lost and are going nowhere they don't know that you already
found your way. that you wander earth how you choose. to the
fullest. outside the box. in the wild. not confined or to the tune
of society. if you were to leave or vanish or go elsewhere off radar
off grid off social media they would be the ones to feel lost. be lost.
be missing part of their heart. so much of you is the light that light
looks to in deference. in solidarity.

the best kind of humans.

the best kind of humans strive to do good. be good. want good. create good. and accept others for who they are because that is what good humans do. find the good ones and cherish their light.

you are a good one. a great one. the greatest one. beautiful light. the best hands down and hearts open. how you can be so good when what is around you can feel so bad and dismal and harsh and heavy. fluid must be beneath your feet as it seems you just float and don't allow nonsense to knock you down. this doesn't mean you avoid the harsh or the hardship. it means you engage in what is challenging and still remain the shape and color of love. only the great ones have this power. this ability. this grace. that is you. grace. hope. endearing. not just willing to do what serves and is right for others. but you are this in action. in motion. in movement. this is what has always set you apart. you never get stuck in words because you are not even needing any backup because your passion and purpose and focus is on doing. on working. on being. so don't get down on yourself if someone asks where you have been or misunderstand anything about you. some just don't know you even if they know you. not everyone can cherish what they themselves don't cherish in them. so be what you know yourself to be. a human of such complexity. not needing verification for the good you know you provide.

four types of love you need.

physical love. touch. closeness. presence.
mental love. understanding. thought provoking.
emotional love. feeling seen. connected. wanted.
spiritual love. chemistry. energy. meaning.

go where this is fostered and grown.
leave where this is nowhere to be found.
you deserve to be flooded with love
not searching for dried up wells.

this is how you know they don't care.

they tell you to get over it.
they think one day)if that(is enough time to grieve.
they get defensive and dismissive.
they blame you for feeling anything but happy.
they go back to business as usual.
they don't ask how they can support you.
they assume you can process by yourself.
they do not prioritize mental health/wellness.
they expect you to hold it together when you just need time to
collect the pieces you didn't shatter. if they aren't there for you in
moments you most need they never will be. protect yourself from
people who love only when it is on their terms and comfortable
and convenient.

heart on lockdown.

that wall you have built not just anyone can surmount. talking through it even the almost deserving ones drought and turn back. but that tells you you're still in process. in healing. in discovering. anyone can wall down and let someone truly not worthy in but without being on lockdown you wouldn't know who or what you are allergic too. don't let anyone tell you to let your guard down just so they can ambush you and end up hurting you due to their own impatience.

the time is y:ou.

the time is y:ou which means you decide what guides you by listening to your intuition. listening to your internal. your spirit has its own watch. y:ou. you owe yourself some time back. you have been acccumulating so much of it by not giving it to you that you can't ever use all of it. but now and now and now and now and not later you must dip into that heart account of yours and spend you on you with you for you. not another hold off and roll it over to next year or next month or next weekend. even next day is too far away. next should be now. as you breathe this. be this. take you in. y:ou o'clock should be carved out daily. part of your practice. intentionally. begin doing this by saying this is my time. do not bother me unless it is absolutely necessary. y:ou time is not selfish it is not selfish it is not selfish it is not selfish it is not selfish.

remove what doesn't serve you.

they can't see it. neither can you. but you are growing. changing. making moves without notice. without shouting out loud. you can feel the difference. in your walk. in the language you use. your sight is different. some catch on and others are clueless. and that's okay. soul work and digging deep isn't for display. that heart of yours hurts for the heart it used to be. the heart that was numb is long gone. you've lost people who you once called friend. called close. called significant. but they were never ready for caring for anyone else. true love takes constant priming and consistency. and that love you have that is brewing over is no longer on tap for childish ones.

even your shadow is light.

even your shadow is light. it is following the direction of the sun. because no matter where you are. wherever you point your energy. your soul is full of sunshine and moonshine and heartshine and loveshine and your beautful reflection is just particles wanting so badly to get back to your hue. back to your home. back to your honey. the vibes of you peak of gold that hint your skin. no wonder when the sky goes black the sky god keeps one eye open to help you remember who you are.

let them deserve you.

you have the biggest heart. you bravely share without question. without reservation. even when you know the giving will get nothing. you steep ino people and tend to always be ten moves ahead with an unreturnable love. how hard it is to give and give and give and pour and spill and pour and spill and some won't offer you a drop. you try to pull back but your heart doesn't work like that. here. dear giver. dear everest of all things good and gift. you touch and change and transform lives. you are extraordinary. remarkable. essential. essential. essential. you are the prayer and the answer. the remedy. the giver. the drain and the drained. use that power on you sometimes. let them search for you. let them deserve you.

moon eyes.

in you there is moon. all moon. full moon. half moon. and you're especially vibrant always. not just every once in a while. always. and even though your mood shifts. your moon never does. it hangs weightless and effortless not timidly but boldly. in wait but not waiting. not for just anyone or anything. you have this plan about you. this balance about you. that illuminates. that waters. that inspires. from up close. from way up high across across. people dare not blink. they can not blink. for in you there is moon. their reminder. their motivation. their guidance. their hope. their ambition. their desire. all in your eyes. just by looking at you they can see you're about love. and if they can tell all of that and feel all of that and want all of you. imagine what the other 99 percent of your soul does. there are no words. just a bunch of countless sighs. deep impact. deep impressions. deep admiration. you are deeper than deep and that's just one glimpse of your moon eyes.

most authentic soul.

you are the most authentic soul i know.
so why do you keep checking others when
it is your glow they want more than their own.

without the weight of someone else's gravity.

now that you are done
comparing yourself
did you notice
how more elegant
how more light
how more present
you are
without
the weight
of someone else's
gravity
holding you down.

spread love.

spread love. spread peace. spread joy. spread hope. spread grace. spread happiness. spread good. spread positivity. spread kindness. spead courage. spread smiles. keep doing this because this is what you have always been about since every breath you have taken. we need more. not from you. from others. just by doing and being you you mirror for others who need the reminder to do and be better. why better. how better. when better. where better. you can transfer where others get blocked. somehow you unstop any blockage any blockage any barrier with simple questions simple requests simple nudges that gently de-escalate and gets results no one else has ever been able to do. it is in the love you spread. you are who love turns to when love needs guidance.

unbothered.

people say over and over not to worry about what others say or think or feel about you. but you are human. and you care that they are okay. even if they treat you like they don't care. that doesn't mean you are in their life. you've mastered the boundary vibes. you know whose mind and heart that matter most and know to be unbothered by the rest. unbothered by what is out of your control. unbothered by who tries to pull because you just keep going where you were heading in the first place. but every blue moon. every so often something hits like lightning into your soul. a word. a comment. a misunderstanding. it can come from nowhere or from the same person who constantly gives you hardship. because the human in you has feelings you get down in wanting to rectify. to make better. to clarify. to defend. to restore. but sometimes there is nothing you can do no matter your language. no matter your tone. no matter your heart. and you can tell yourself to be unbothered but it hurts your sensibilities. in your heart space. because you do so much. give so much. care so much. want to always be in a good place. and then your unbothered mantra recalibrates. switches back to make sense to protect your essence. it's okay to be unbothered and be bothered ever so often. your skin isn't made of teflar. it gives your heart loving practice to express its depths.

unhide the hidden ones.

in one moment)slice of a moment(you can make a person feel what someone who has been in their life for a million moments never could make them feel. call it being seen. call it being loved. call it being understood. you are what so many lovers wish they had. wish they met first. wish they knew personally. heartfully. wholefully. soulfully. mindfully. lipsfully. intimately. it is as if you place your hand over the tender parts. the wounded parts. the hurt spots. and untwist them. carefully. lovingly. patiently. gently. then all at once. allowing souls to begin again. to forget they blamed themselves for all the pain they carried around. inside. outside. oh how they wish they collided with you first. before all the sharp edges of love and loss breached their world. for coming across you first would have protected them. but you give them a second chance. by accepting them as they are. when they breathe it is like new breath. when they see it is like new sight. when they make love it is like new love. you do that. make people feel comfortable in themselves. you unhide the hidden ones and create a safe space for everyone to be authentically them.

wildfire.

you are a fire no one can contain. always ablaze always fiery always fearless. the light of you is never dim or dull or goes out. it ignites. it lights. it scorches the plains in others and rises high)so high(the stars above stars can feel your burn. at times you look soft and delicate but that is because you are made up of flowers and honey. you are a wildfire. created from the earth's core mixed with beauty. mixed with unstoppable. mixed with flame. smoke means you are somewhere nearby. but sometimes you forget. sometimes you leave your fire inside the house as you leave for the day. someone sometimes tells you you're too hot. too much. and you put yourself out. you put yourself down. but wildfire you're supposed to burn and be bold and be what makes even the dullest shine. you would be the one to accomodate and just be a pilot light)a small flame(but stay big and blaze. you are responsible for all that new growth. new life. new energy. new mentality. new opportunity. new love. remember that you are both necessary and dangerous. people resist wanting to be around others who naturally turn everything and everyone into gold. keep making gold. remain wildfire always.

why they leave.

because they were never for you.

love is your crown.

love is your crown. it is the lens from which you see. the chords
from which your voice breathes. the religion you practice. the
energy that steps into each step you take and the alarm you wake
to. don't take it off. don't turn it down. don't set it on a shelf and
have it collect dust and replace it with anything else. no update
necessary. no service or tune-up only a tune-in. stay present to
it. with it. stand by it. many will try to knock who you are to rile
you up and irritate and prove you're just like them. and you are
like them because you have a heart but their heart is no where
near yours. yours would never intentionally damage someone. you
are royal because of that love inside you. that gold giver in you.
that fast yes instead of slow maybe. and even as you put up with
drama of life at home or at school or at work or wherever you find
yourself that love filter holds so much. collects so much. it seems
you take it with you. them with you. their stuff. their worry. their
heavy. their unrest. their story. and far too many times think it is
on you to fix. or change. or hold. or bury. as if you are the reason
they are in agony. as if by changing you they will get some relief.
but you can't change you in hopes to change anything in someone
else. that isn't fair and it isn't on you to believe you have to always
take on what others try to stick and pin and latch onto you. all that
isn't your responsibility. but you can send them with love. think of
them in love. hope for them in love. that is always your routine.
just stop allowing any more negative thorns pierce your skin. of
course sometimes it is for you to take in if you were in the wrong
or did something out of your awareness that ended up hurting
feelings or making matters worse. whatever makes you better do
that. breathe that in. let that in. that other stuff has no business
near your energy because love is your crown and anything less
than love should be denied access.

the most beautiful human.

you see the beauty in others and that makes you
the most beautiful human.

the best type of happiness.

the best type of happiness rests in small places. in the tiniest
places. in the tiniest less obvious spaces. you miss it if you look too
hard. you lose it when you doubt you have it or compare what you
have found to the tide of others. the best type of happiness is when
you can see your own water. feel it's powerful depth and proclaim:
i am enough. i am enough.

nothing shallow is allowed near you.

you remind breath to breathe deeper. love to love deeper. heart to heart deeper. soul to soul deeper. kisses to kiss deeper. tides to tide deeper. nothing shallow is allowed near you.

your reach is beyond your control.

you never know who looks for and needs your light. that's not your style. you don't seek recognition and nor does light. nor does moon. nor does sky. nor does star. you can't help but be sought after and emulated. so be you. you beautiful light. beautiful moon. even at your lowest you shine bright. keep your energy)all that cosmic mind blowing heart opening energy(away from wishing souls would stop copying you. watching you. eyeing you. tracking you. taking taking taking taking taking taking taking taking taking. believe it or not the moon will always be moon. sun will always be sun. love will always be love. so always be you. accept that others look in your direction. look in your shadow. look at the little things just to capture a glimpse of incredible. a glimpse of ooh. a glimpse of goosebumps. a glimpse of you. too much time on trying to keep glances off you takes you from you. your ness. your more important things. by being you and focusing on you you get closer and closer and closer to the enlightenment that is meant for you. this isn't the season to worry about who is doing what you are doing. let them be on their path to find their way and right now their way is learning from you how it is done. how it can be done. so rise and rise and rise and rise and blur anything that isn't going to help get you where you need to go. see it as an honor that your growth serves as a beacon. and beacons can't dictate what they touch. for your reach is beyond your control.

the greatest love.

the type of love that changes your life.
you already have it. you already are it.
there is no doubt you're the greatest love.

attached.

somehow you make detachment look so easy. but it's not. holding on to people and to memories and to old love is what most do. but you don't. you can let go. you can move on. you believe that no one belongs to no one. that just as you are a free bird any soul that sets in your sights is free, too. super free. can do what they will. no attachments. because those bind us. and you don't want to be bound or tied down or told what you can and cannot do. you choose to love who you choose to love in moments that feel like forever to them. but it's just an instant to you. because your love slows time. and anyone in that moment who happens to have your heart experiences what they have never been able to feel in their entire lifetime. it is unreal. unspeakable. you give good love. the greatest love. a hypnotic love. but you don't want them obsessed)they can't help it(. for you detachment doesn't mean you don't care it means you let go of control. you don't want to be with someone just for the sake of being with someone. you want them to be their independent self just as you are your own independent self. you don't need their validation but require their acceptance. for you are you. and they are they. and where most get caught up in what relationships mean in terms of defining, you cannot and do not want to be defined or denied or dictated to. your detachment is an attachment to a need to draw your own boundaries. you are your own. you wouldn't have it any other way.

twenty signs you're a beautiful giver.

the sun sets on your cue.
you are unaware of the fireworks you create in others.
you have a tendency to overextend. overshare. overcare.
overkind. overfeel. overthink. overlove.
you release love without question.
taking isn't in your vocabulary.
you are an endless lover.
the world blooms for you.
people heal different around you.
you sometimes feel abandoned and misunderstood.
everyone searches for you.
there when no one expects it.
you are a lot of things to a lot of people.

let them go. keep yourself.

and sometimes trying harder doesn't work. trying harder makes things worse. you tense up and rush. you push yourself for the sake of what you think others want from you. and in the end they are the ones who aren't trying. they are off the hook. and you are left spinning your wheels and fighting twice more than you should. but this is you. you try and try and try and try. but for a moment just try less and be. be present to the why you might be trying so hard. and listen for a response. not saying you should give up. but sometimes doing the work for two leaves you burnt out on a lost cause. and sometimes you need to let go of souls who just don't care. it's okay to let them go. and keep yourself.

lace.

anything from you is laced with love.

four flowers to give yourself.

grace. be gentle. it's okay to not be okay.
permission. to break. to cry. to take up space.
affirmation. all the words you need to hear.
water. music. bath. whatever brings you joy.

protect your peace.
as much as you can.
give all the love and
all the attention and
all that that you want
from others to yourself.
don't feel guilty for
needing time to
refuel.
give what you always
give beautifully.
you.

peaceful love.

you are a peaceful love. the kind that wraps. that holds. that warms. that nourishes. that grows. all at once. never stop your love for anyone who can't appreciate your love. who can't add to your element. who can't stand your entire experience and blast their disdain their resent their negative vibration as there is no space big enough to entertain those whose energy isn't complementary or sufficient or harmonious. the time for imbalance is gone. nothing and no one should rip you away from the work you are committed to. the growth you are focused on. the best version you are trying to be. those not going with you might mean they just aren't ready for soul work but you can't stay. your peace is too essential to wait. too necessary to neglect. too healing to halt. so when it gets to be too much you will have you. and all of that peaceful presence. and all of that deep love. how it must be to be you. to be so effortlessly beautiful in your skin.

you are water.

you are water.
powerful enough to drown.
soft enough to cleanse.
deep enough to save.

and when people come to you they have no choice. no option. no way around. the skyline of you is far above their sea level. there is nothing to deny or shy away from when naming and stating that you are above the rest. not above as in better. but above on a spiritual plane. it is intimidating only in that souls know you are no nonsense. all the small and big things that are done have meaning. nothing is empty because you make it full. make it excess. make it spill. your very presence is the permission one only needs to deeply care. not shallow care. there is a difference. you shine your whole being into people. they can feel the weight of your greatness. the gravity of your softness. the scent of your freshness. so many look to you as if you are the perfect one. the one with plans but you are furthest from the pedestal they put you on. you actually sink it whenever it is brought up because that's not how you live. up there. wherever there is. you're grounded. under ground. in the earth. in the mud. in the water. splashing. tinkering. figuring out. all of this may sound repititive but that is life. constant rotation. coming back on to itself. you come back and try and do better the next go round. the stories have different characters but the theme remains the same and you pick up quickly on lessons and breadcrumbs and intuition from before. that makes you water. makes you reservoir and tank and bearer and holder of what becomes and what grows. it comes from you because you aren't representative you are source. so when souls come to you they automatically heal and breathe and sigh. you are water.

the day before and the day after.

you are the day before and the day after. experiencing you is the calm and the rush. the first time wonder and all time magic felt so deeply in the soul. you are what others need. you are everything you need. everything everything. you just have to breathe yourself in more. it's okay to give you some of you every now and then. make that now rather than later. so when you are down down down let your down days be when you love on yourself harder.

xo.

there are no words. not enough of them anyway. to pull out. to decide to use. to articulate the realm of you. all things are possible but you are everimpossible to drill down. and that is the point. the argument. the ruling. to convince you of how unfeasible it is to sojourn and bring back to you anything meaningful. because even that isn't deep enough. this volume didn't come close. nor the one before. but it is never a waste of breath to venture to pour at your feet the trying. the uncovering. the work. not to prove or to earn or swoon but to mirror and show some resemblance of you that you can see. some idea that may get you to see what it is that others see. for what others can't articulate. for when there are lowest lows and you pull this from your nightstand you can take a hit of this and breathe some love back into any insecurity or doubt or difficulty. to equalize you. to bring your smile back. to embrace you to know that someone feels you. needs you. loves loves loves loves loves loves loves loves loves loves loves loves loves you. you. beautiful giver. need to be raised and celebrated and shouted about over and over for all the countless all the wonderful all the deep care and patience and small acts of kindess you root into the earth of others. what an anchor you are. it feels too much because you deplete yourself. you know no different so this isn't an ask to do anything other than this: sit. or stand. drop your shoulders. close your eyes or gaze them somewhere. focus and listen to your breath. inhale. exhale. notice all the sensations of your body. connect with your body. and while you are there. while you communicate softly with whatever comes up this is most important. thank yourself. truly. affirm yourself. whatever that means. whatever feels necessary. cry words you need to hear. re-heart yourself. re-soul. re-turn to you. you are the reason. the season of you is at high tide. dear moon. and when you are ready read these words again. xo.

Made in the USA
Columbia, SC
02 August 2020

14487147R00105